Joe Lion's BIG BOOTS

KARA MAY

Illustrated by
JONATHAN ALLEN

KING*f*ISHER

To Marian & Isobel
& Alasdair – J.A.

KINGFISHER

An imprint of Kingfisher Publications Plc
New Penderel House, 283-288 High Holborn
London WC1V 7HZ

First published by Kingfisher 2000
4 6 8 10 9 7 5 3
TS1/1103/AJT/FR/115SMA

A CIP catalogue record for this book
is available from the British Library.

ISBN 0 7534 0409 5

Printed in India

Contents

Chapter One

Joe Lion was small.

He was the smallest in his class.

He couldn't even reach

to feed the goldfish.

"It's only me who

can't reach,"

said Joe.

He was the smallest in his family, too.

Big Brother Ben could reach

the biscuit jar, easy peasy.

Sister Susan could reach it

easy peasy, too.

But Joe? He couldn't reach it,

not even on tiptoe.

"I'm fed up with being small,"

he said to Mum and Dad.

"I was small once," said Dad.

"You'll grow bigger one day,"

Mum told him.

But Joe wanted to be bigger NOW.

"I'll WISH myself bigger," he said.

He shut his eyes and wished.

He was still wishing when

he went to bed.

But the next morning, he was

the same small Joe Lion.

"Wishing hasn't made me bigger," he said.

"I'll have to think of something else."

He went to the big comfy chair

where he did his thinking.

But what was this on the chair?

 It was Mum's new book,

How to Grow Sunflowers.

"Aha!" grinned Joe.

"That gives me an idea."

Big Brother Ben had a *How to . . .*

book – just the book Joe wanted.

He raced up to Ben's room.

On the bed he saw the book:

How to Build Yourself a Bigger Body.

Joe read through it in a flash.

To get bigger, he had to eat

lots of food like pasta.

Mmm! Yum!

"I have to work out, too," said Joe.

"I know where I can do that!"

Chapter Two

Joe ran all the way to Gus Gorilla's gym.

Gus was big. Very big!

"Working out seems to do the trick,"

thought Joe.

"I can't wait to start," he said to Gus.

"What do I have to do?"

"You stand on this and run!" said Gus.

Joe ran on the running machine.

Then it was onto the exercise bike.

After that, it was the rowing machine.

"Now, lift these weights, young Joe,"
said Gus. "Lift them good and high."

Joe's arms ached. His legs ached.

Even his little finger ached!

But he wanted to be bigger.

He picked up the weights.

He lifted them good and high . . .

until a weight fell –

CRASH!

"Yikes! It nearly hit my foot. That's the
end of working out for me," said Joe.
But he was still determined to get bigger.

"Now I'm not working out," said Joe, "I'll do lots of extra eating to make up for it." Wherever Joe went, whatever Joe was doing, it was: MUNCH! CRUNCH! GOBBLE! At home:

MUNCH! CRUNCH! GOBBLE!

At school:

MUNCH! CRUNCH! GOBBLE!

On the bus:

MUNCH! CRUNCH! GOBBLE!

Even in the bath:

MUNCH! CRUNCH! GOBBLE!

"I must be bigger by now,"
said Joe at last. He went to
have a look in the mirror.
He didn't like what he saw.
"Oh no," he groaned. After
all that working out and
eating, he was bigger, yes!
Bigger-WIDER!

"But I want to be bigger-TALLER!"
said Joe.

Sister Susan had got bigger-taller
in just five minutes.

He asked her how she did it.

"I put on my high-heeled shoes,"
she said.

"Aha!" said Joe.

"That gives me an idea . . .!"

Chapter Three

Joe rushed into Ernie Elephant's shoe shop.
"I need some shoes to make me
bigger-taller," he said.
"Boots are best for that," said Ernie.
Joe tried on lots of boots, but none
of them made him as bigger-taller
as he wanted.

"I can make you some," said Ernie.
"But it'll cost you, AND it's money
in advance."
Joe paid Ernie. "It's all the money
I've got, but it will be worth it,"
said Joe.
"I'll bring them round – delivery
is free," said Ernie.

Joe couldn't wait
for the new boots
to arrive.
But at last, here was
Ernie. Now for the
BIG MOMENT.

Joe took the lid off the box.
He took out his new boots and
put them on.
"This is more like it!" said Joe.
He went to show the others.
"Surprise, surprise!
I'm lots bigger-taller now."
They were surprised all right –
too surprised to speak!

Bigger-taller Joe could do lots of things he couldn't do before.

He could reach the hall light. He turned it on and off – just because he could!

He could reach the rope to swing from.

He could see over Gus Gorilla's fence.

His new boots made a great noise, too!

CLUMP! CLUMP! CLUMP!

"I'll call them my Clumping Clumpers," said Joe.

"That's a good name for them," said Mum.

But the next morning, Mum said, "You can't wear those things to school!"

"I've *got* to wear them," said Joe. In his Clumping Clumpers he wouldn't be the smallest in the class.

"I feel like an ant that's turned into a giant," he said, as he set off down the path.

Today was going to be his best school day ever!

Chapter Four

Joe made his way to the bus stop.

"I like this bigger-taller me!"

he said.

He was closer to the

sky, and could feel

the sun better.

He saw the bus coming,

and ran to catch it – or tried to!

In his Clumping Clumpers he could

only: CLUMP! CLUMP! CLUMP!

The bus went without him.

Joe was late for school.

Mrs Croc wasn't pleased.

"I'm sorry, Mrs Croc," said Joe.

"It was my Clumping Clumpers."

"Can I feed the goldfish?" he asked.

But the goldfish was already fed.

At break, his mates were playing
football. Joe was good at scoring goals.

But not in his Clumping Clumpers.

Joe was glad to get home.

"Biscuit jar, here I come!"

He reached it, easy peasy.

Now to watch his favourite television

programme, *Super Lion in Space*.

But then Mum said, "Hang up your

coat, Joe. You can reach the hook

in your Clumping Clumpers."

And that was just the start of it.

Joe could reach lots of things he
couldn't reach when he was small
Joe Lion.

Like the kitchen sink:

"You can take a turn at washing up,"
said Big Brother Ben.

Like the toy shelf:

"You can put your toys up there

yourself," said Sister Susan.

Washing up! Tidying up!

"It's all I seem to do these days!"

said Joe.

But he couldn't do much else

in his Clumping Clumpers.

Later, Joe's mates were off to the park.

"Are you coming, Joe?" they asked.

Joe shook his head.

He couldn't join in the games.

"I can only clump!" he said.

"I'm off for a walk."

Joe clumped off down the street.

CLUMP! CLUMP! CLUMP!

But what was up with Geoff Giraffe?

"He looks like he's in trouble!"

said Joe.

Chapter Five

Joe soon discovered that Geoff

WAS in trouble.

"Daffy giraffe that I am,

I've locked myself out," he said.

"I came outside to pick some flowers,

and I left the bath running!"

Joe saw the problem at once.

Left to itself the bath would overflow

and Geoff's house would be flooded!

Joe spotted the bathroom window –
it was open!

"You can get in up there," he said.

Geoff got his head in.

"But my bottom half won't fit,"
said Geoff. "The window's too small."

"Leave this to me," said Joe.

He knew what he must do.
First, off with his Clumping
Clumpers.

Now, it was
Super Joe Lion
to the rescue!
Up the drainpipe.
In through the
window.

The water was rising fast —

and lots of soapy bubbles with it!

"I must act at once!" Joe reached

for the plug.

It was too far down.

He would have to go in!

He got up on the side of the bath

and jumped.

SPLASH!

He couldn't see through the bubbles
and his breath was running out.
But he must get to the plug.
"Got it!" He pulled the plug and
out it came.
The water gurgled down.
GLUG! GLUG! GLUG!
Joe whooshed the bubbles
out the window.

Then he skimmed back down
the drainpipe.
He saw a crowd had gathered.
Mum and Dad were there, and
Brother Ben and Sister Susan
and Gus and Ernie and
Mrs Croc and all his mates.
They were waiting for news.

Quickly, Joe told them:

"Geoff's house is safe from flooding
by bath water and it's safe from
bubbles, too!"

They all gave a cheer.

"Hurrah for Super Joe Lion!"

Joe felt very proud.

He was Super Joe Lion – just

as he was. He didn't need his

Clumping Clumpers.

"My clumping days are over," said Joe. "Being me is best. I don't want to be bigger . . . Well, not yet!"

About the Author and Illustrator

Kara May was born in Australia, and as a child she acted on the radio. She says, "Even though I am grown-up now, I am still the smallest in my family, so I know just how Joe Lion feels." Kara used to work in the theatre and has written lots of plays for children, but now she writes books full-time.

Jonathan Allen played bass guitar in a band before he graduated from Art School. He says, "When I was young I wanted to be a famous rock star, like the one in the poster on Brother Ben's bedroom wall." Now Jonathan is well known for illustrating children's books . . . but he does still play his bass guitar!

If you've enjoyed reading *Joe Lion's Big Boots,*
try these other **I Am Reading** books:

ALLIGATOR TAILS AND CROCODILE CAKES
Nicola Moon & Andy Ellis

BARN PARTY
Claire O'Brien & Tim Archbold

THE GIANT POSTMAN
Sally Grindley & Wendy Smith

GRANDAD'S DINOSAUR
Brough Girling & Stephen Dell

JJ RABBIT AND THE MONSTER
Nicola Moon & Ant Parker

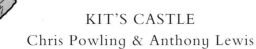

KIT'S CASTLE
Chris Powling & Anthony Lewis

MISS WIRE AND THE THREE KIND MICE
Ian Whybrow & Emma Chichester Clark

MR COOL
Jacqueline Wilson & Stephen Lewis

MRS HIPPO'S PIZZA PARLOUR
Vivian French & Clive Scruton

PRINCESS ROSA'S WINTER
Judy Hindley & Margaret Chamberlain

WATCH OUT, WILLIAM
Kady MacDonald Denton